novum pro

AF066436

J.N.S. Pluckrose

Thringer –
The beginning of a great tale

novum pro

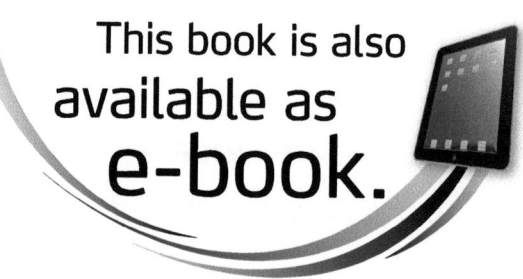

www.novum-publishing.co.uk

All rights of distribution, including via film, radio, and television, photomechanical reproduction, audio storage media, electronic data storage media, and the reprinting of portions of text, are reserved	© 2016 novum publishing ISBN 978-3-99048-468-5 Editing: Louise Darvid Cover photo: J.N.S. Pluckrose Cover design, layout & typesetting: novum publishing Internal illustrations: J.N.S. Pluckrose (9)
Printed in the European Union on environmentally friendly, chlorine- and acid-free paper.	**www.novum-publishing.co.uk**

Chapter 1
The Start

Any story has a world and that world is a lump of clay that will be moulded throughout the chapters of this book.

The world of Thringer has edges; this world is like a huge dinner dish where the ever flowing sea will forever fall in to the mists. With many places around Thringer; Atlantis the oldest and wisest, more wise than the elves of the magic wood. The dragon isles, a place that is unventured for it had a high number of dragons making it their home in the caves and craters that the island has to offer. Also keeping it a safe place where dragons can mate and lay eggs.

A frozen prison of doom on the frozen lands of Block, a cursed land of large ice rocks always moving making it impossible to map or explore, so its hosts the place of exiled.

The hidden island, home to traitors and smugglers hidden from the world by a veil of densest mist.

There may be many battles and wars but overall the world is one of peace, as flowers will bloom and rivers will run with crystal clear water trickling down from the massive rocky slopes of giant mountains. The green grass covering fields, farms filled with corn and towns filled with people. This world is filled with many people and animals. There was much trading and conversing between each and every town and kingdom. Most trading was done from Mount Moon with the Dwarf city where the masters of steel created great weapons, many of them to be sold from the Handel Islands. This was the perfect world but the powers of dark magic was creeping back, corrupting the peace, leaving Thringer a broken world.

In the land were many types of life; Man, a creature with no limit but doomed to die. Ninja, are men who have great skills, the best at hunting and hiding, masters of the shadows. Elves, immortal, descendent from angels sent to the land to be its protectors. Viking, masters of war, brought up in very tough conditions. Dwarfs, the descendents of Viking's; the men that were too weak were left on land and were soon the masters of steel. Pirate's, masters of the sea, but had a large obsession for treasure and shiny things. There are many more creatures, but I will tell you about them when we find them in our story.

    For the creation of this world, no one knows the great story of formation. Except for Atlantis they are the only people who know, but they keep away from the world. They are to guard the information with their lives for the evils that could be revealed. In the creation many hills and mountains were formed at the beginning of time. The only other clue to how the world was formed is The Great Stone. This stone, was no normal stone, it had a great power to form or destroy anything. That is when the trouble began, because of it's great power and unknown contents, it stayed in the one mountain called Striff. This mountain stood alone surrounded by Great Plains of sand and dust, no life a terrible place, even more terrible in the stone war. For each kingdom wanted the stone's great power for themselves. So the armies were built and went to the mountain of Striff; the yellow plains of Striff were soon turned red. The Stone War was a long two years of nothing but bloodshed.

    There were many armies to fight, every person on the land of Thringer fought for their lives. There were many races to fight in this war, one of the races was an evil mess of dark creatures, led by an immortal man who has been around as long as the land itself. He was once a member of Atlantis until he was chased out. He went by the name of Gergriff. He was only one of a few that was around at the start of time. He had an evil race of monsters and goblins born from black magic to do his bidding.

    All fought in the war, all but the three kings, they stayed in their kingdoms away from the war. They built The Tor a massive wall of stone winding and cutting through a massive range of mountains. Which broke them from the main land, there they stayed, never going in to war or helping the people of Thringer. They watched as the world died.

    As I said before, the Stone War went on for a bad two years. Thousands and thousands, too many to count were killed in the slaughter. Until it came to the Last Day each great leader from each kingdom, each of them walked in to the Mountain of Striff. They were ready for the final fight.

There was a great monastery built by Monks to show their respect to The Great Stone. In the Last Day that building was no more than rubble. The leaders each made their way in to the Stone room. In the centre of the room was a golden altar, hosting the great stone, no bigger than a rabbit. The room's walls were rich with gold and jewels placed there by the Monks.

In that room the last fight of The Stone War took place between the leaders. They fought until the stone glowed a green glow and a crystal table formed from the ground and engulfed the Stone in blue light. The men were confused but there was no more time to fight for the table blasted up straight through the mountain, smashing it to pieces. Striff exploded like a volcano without lava, the stone floated one mile in the air over Striff. The battles stopped, all the people of Thringer looked up at the explosion. Large chunks of crystal fell back in to the mountain, large rocks dropped from the sky crushing and killing parts of the army. The stone then broke itself in to five pieces. Each part let out a blast of light as they bolted through the air like meteors and they smashed down in front of each of the main armies or what was left of them.

On this event the Stone splitting the kingdoms formed a truce never to have another war like The Stone War.

The Stone's great power was then used wisely by each kingdom for the Stone has the power to create. The men used their stone to build the great fortress of Vocar. The Elves built a city in to a mountain, deep within the Magic Wood. Ninjas built their home up in the trees of another forest, a large entanglement of modular houses and walkways. The Vikings built a great port to live and trade in, but for Gergriff this power was not enough, even though he was trusted with one of the stones. He built a great tower of black magic where in secret, he was going to rebuild his army and start another war to engulf the land.

"And that, children, is how it all started", said the teacher.

We come from the past to a library in Vocar where a teacher has just read a group of students the start of time, a great book written by the first king.

"That was great", said Henry. Henry was sitting in the back row of the class; he was a student that enjoyed the tales of Thringer.

"I'm glad you liked that", said the Teacher. "I will see you all tomorrow, we will be starting the next topic", she said.

The students picked up their sacks and bags, got up and walked to the door of the library. Henry was the last to get up. He pulled up a book and put it in his bag but as he walked out a voice called out to him.

"You there", said a voice from the near table.

Henry stopped and looked around to see an old man dressed in a long dark blue robe. In his hands he held up a large white book. He had a very long white beard and a head bald except for a little blue hat; he wore a black belt with a golden hook and a brown case for his sword.

"Are you Henry, son?" asked the old man.

"Yes", said Henry. Turning and walking to the old man.

"Your father asked me to tutor you", said the old man sitting down on one of the long brown tables.

"I see", said Henry getting slowly closer.

"Take a seat, this will be fun" said the old man. He opened the book to page one and then looked up to see Henry sitting.

"We'll start with a read of Thringer history", said the old man.

"Ready?" asked the old man.

"Yes, sir", said Henry.

The old man began to read.

In a city of grey stone, the houses made of wood and filled with people, food and animals. This is the city of Vocar where peace would reign. A wall around the city to keep the town safe, large golden gates made of strong oak. In the centre of the city was a great citadel; home and stronghold of the king Oring. This castle, built to defend against any kind of attack, built tall with massive towers with large blue cones on the tallest towers, many stained glass windows with patterns of people, old kings and knights.

On this day it just happened to be a coronation, up on one of the floors in one of the rooms.

Origer, son of Oring, he was being dressed ready by his servant Beakey; he was being dressed in his ceremonial armour.

"Come on, Beakey", said Origer, fussing.

Origer, the young prince of Vocar, the boy who hated the idea that he would have to run the kingdom some day. His head filled with adventure and skilled with a sword. His mother died when Origer was 7, his father and the servants then had to raise him as best they could, for a mother and son have a great bond. Origer had hit the age of 20 and today he was going to be made the prince of Vocar. He was dressed in green robes and silver armour with the crest of Vocar. The crest was a picture of a large amount of flowers around a sword closing around the blade which was to show that swords are not the answer for peace. Origer's face had a short brown beard with dark brown hair, he had blue eyes and a scar just under his neck.

"Hold still", said Beakey, who was clipping on his armour.

Beakey's story was a mystery to many; most of his past was hidden. The only thing that is known was that he was a pirate, until he showed up in Vocar looking for work.

Beakey was dressed in a green servant uniform, simple green shirt with a small crest at the top left corner and brown trousers with large black boots. He had a brown beard but it was a lot longer than Origer, his beard came down to his chest, it would be longer, but Beakey had golden hooks and clips in it to make it look respectable.

"Done", said Beakey stepping back to look at his work.

"Well… you're getting better", said Origer looking at himself in the mirror. He looked at the armour and then he noticed something.

"Beakey?" asked Origer.

"Yes, sire?" asked Beakey.

"Beakey, what is this?" said Origer. He turned holding his belt and he pushed up the sword case to show it empty.

"I'm surprised you've forgotten, that is a sword case, sire", said Beakey.

"What is missing?" said Origer, getting very angry at this point.

"It is missing… don't tell me… urr… don't tell me… I know this, got it, it is missing the sword", said Beakey.

"Well", said Origer.

"Your sword, yes, I put it, I put it here", said Beakey walking back to the table looking for it to see that it had fallen to the floor. He picked it up and put it in Origer's case.

Origer then looked at Beakey, he picked up a candle (nothing else to grab).

"Do that again and…" said Origer, gesturing the candle at Beakey.

"You're threatening me with a candle", said Beakey.

Origer at this point very angry, was going to hit him when a KNOCK, KNOCK came from his door.

"Yes?" said Origer putting the candle down. Now Beakey could get up from the floor.

The door opened and another servant walked in "You have five minutes sire", said the servant.

"Right", said Origer.

The servant left and Origer took a deep breath and looked at himself in the mirror.

"It's time", said Origer.

"Yes, sire", said Beakey.

"Beakey you're the person who knows me the best. Will I make a good prince?" said Origer.

"Truth?" asked Beakey.

"Truth", said Origer.

"Well, I think… you'll do good", said Beakey.

"Right then, let's go", said Origer. He walked up to the doors, opening them. They both walked down the hall until they came to a set of giant doors. Two guards pulled them open and Origer stood looking in to see massive crowds of people, looking at him. There was a long red carpet going down through the middle of the room up to the throne where the king was waiting. Origer started to walk, as he walked, the people would bow. They were all dressed in posh and fine clothes.

While at the back of the room, Beakey slipped in to the servant's space.

"Hello", said Beakey tapping one of the ladies on the shoulder.

"Hello, Beakey", she said. This was Sandy. She was a servant that helped Beakey to become a servant, to teach him the ropes; tricks of the trade as they say.

"What do you think of my work?" asked Beakey.

"It's great", said Sandy. Looking at Origer's cloak from which Beakey had removed a bad mud stain.

"How did you remove that stain?" asked Sandy.

"Paint", said Beakey.

"Paint? You dozy thing", said Sandy looking back around at the cloak.

Origer walked up three steps, in front of him sat Oring in a large golden throne, in the top of the chair, was the part of the stone that man was given in The Stone War, kept safe in a golden harness.

Oring sat in his throne, in his best golden armour with the same crest, a long red cape with many patterns. On his face was a short white beard and grey hair, on his head he wore a golden crown with many treasures. He was dressed very expensively even for a king.

Origer came up and kneeled in front of the king. He slowly got up and using his staff he walked to his son Origer. At the same time another servant came up with a pillow with a smaller crown on it, filled with jewels.

The king took up the crown and held it over Origer's head.

"My son Origer for the first time, you will be crowned Prince of Vocar. You are to defend Vocar and everyone inside her walls for the rest of your days. Do you swear?"

"I swear", said Origer.

"Do you swear to obey and use the law to its full power?"

"I swear", said Origer.

"Do you swear to keep the great stone safe?"

"I swear", said Origer.

"Do you swear to pass this crown down to your sons?"

"I swear" said Origer

"Then, my son, I dub thee crowned Prince of Vocar", said Oring.

He slowly lowered the crown on to Origer's head. Origer then stood and turned to his people as they clapped and cheered, looking up to their great new leader who would lead them through the dark protected toward the light.

"Long live the prince", said Oring.

"Long live the prince!" shouted the crowd.

"Long live the prince!" shouted the crowd.

"Long live the prince!" shouted the crowd.

Chapter 2
A Bad Night

The day was done and the night began. The throne room alight with lights had been filled with a very long large wooden table. A smell filled the castle, the table covered in all kinds of food. Lots of apples, grapes, pears, pineapples, there was bread and cheese, salted fish, squid, also meat, legs of ham, legs of pork, all types of chops of every size and flavour. On each table was a full fried bore, but still bigger than that was cakes stacked up six layers high, covered in icing. There were buns and jam tarts, cream cakes and chocolate logs, enough to fill an army. At the tables were people in their best dresses or suits, eating the food and laughing at the magic show. There were three men and two women in the centre of the room shooting arrows at each other, chaining up people and locking them in boxes, blowing fire, finding cards and all other sorts of magic tricks.

"The head table at the back of the room had the king, prince and the most important members of council sitting at it. At the end of the table, standing on the table was Glyn, Origer pet wolf. I forgot to tell you about Glyn. Origer found him when he was young and Glyn had lived with Origer for a very long time. He had light grey fur with a white stripe across his stomach. He was enjoying a chicken. Wrapping his large choppers and teeth in to the meat.

"The evening was still young and the guests were having a great time, until DING, DING, DING the sound of the warning bell filled the room. A knight burst in.

"My king, you must see this", he said.

So the knights led Oring and Origer to the wall, they looked out to the forest. From there sprung hundreds of people carrying boxes and bags, barrels and carts, pulling animals, carrying their children. Slowly walking up the path towards the door.

The oak gates opened and the king walked out, straight to see Clut the leader and king of the elves. As another king he was wearing silver armour, he had long brown hair and a wooden crown, on his back was a quiver of arrows, on his belt were two very well made posh blades.

The other person at the door was Claw, queen of the ninjas. She was dressed different again; she had a purple dress with a golden leaf painted on her belt .There were three long thin blades across her chest. There was a string of throwing stars. Hanging from her neck a vile of water from the tree of souls. A tree that the ninja's are to protect for they believe that when people die part of their souls will stay in the tree and keep the land safe. The ninja's have many traditions and events that must take place.

"What brings you here?" asked Oring.

"War, war brings us", said Clut.

"War has begun", said Claw.

"So why are you here, what happened to your homes?" asked Oring.

"Our home is no more than ash", said Claw. "The forest is gone",

"Ours has been burnt also", said Clut.

"Then you will take refuge", said Oring.

"We will stand together", said Oring.

"Son, Captain, get your men, help these people, start filling the courtyard then move through the city. We need all the space we can get", said Oring.

"Yes, Father", said Origer walking off through his men saying, "You men with me",

So the lines of people kept coming out of the forest, across the plains, up the ramp through the door in to the city. Supplies were being stocked in the castle, knights in lines passing one to one to one on a line leading down to the basement. The king had two men taking people's names and counting up numbers. In just two hours, they had over 4,300 new people in the walls of Vocar. Origer and Oring were standing on a balcony, overlooking all the people walking through.

"What do they mean, war?" asked Origer.

"Means we're in trouble", said Oring.

"Not so good then", said Origer.

"No, son, not good at all. Now the elves and ninja have come here, we are the last fortress to stand against Gergriff", said Oring.

"What of the three kings?" asked Origer.

"They won't fight or help. No man has crossed the Tor in 300 years" said Oring.

"At least we're standing together", said Origer.

"Yes... I'm sorry, son. This night was meant to be yours", said Oring.

"It's Ok, Father. To be a good king sacrifices must be made", said Origer.

"Son, you will make a great king", said Oring putting an arm over his son's shoulder and petting Glyn.

More and more came across the plain as servants went out to help them. Beakey walked out to a family pulling a small cart, with two old people asleep in the back. The mother walking with her children, the dad was pulling and looked exhausted, so Beakey walked up and helped to pull the cart.

"Help has arrived", said Beakey.

"Thank you..." puffed and panted the dad, as Beakey pulled them in to the city.

Another two hours passed in to the night, as the total number of people had hit over 27,000. With the greatest luck, they could see the end of the line of people, just coming out of the forest. But that's when the trap sprung. The line had reached halfway across the plain when there came a "scream" from the forest, then the sound of...

"Attack!" shouted a voice. Seconds later a load of Vikings started to pour out of the woods, screaming and shouting their battle cries.

"Vikings!" shouted a guard.

Again the warning bell rang, as soldiers ran through and around the castle, readying weapons and preparing for battle. But as I said the doors were still open and people were starting to run in. Some of the knights and Beakey were helping pull people in, until they saw the attack they drew swords and stood strong ready to hold the Vikings away from the people.

"Move!" shouted a knight pushing and rushing the people along.

People were screaming as they ran up in to the castle. The knights and Beakey trapped on the plain were fighting back.

"There's too many!" shouted a knight.

"Give us a minute", said Beakey, tripping a Viking then stabbing another.

As Beakey and three knights were fighting, hundreds were running past. By then the villagers just got to the gates of Vocar, but the Vikings were only steps behind so as the villagers ran in, the knights ran out to defend as Beakey and his last standing knight walked up the path defending every slice and cut. It was not soon that the last knight was killed. After that Beakey pushed the Viking in front of him and he made a dash for the doors. He ran in and behind the wall it was madness.

"Sharp shooters to the top", said Claw. Walking up to the wall, they started to rain arrows down on the Vikings. Viking blood began to pour over the steps of Vocar. The slaughter of both knight and Viking marked the start of the war.

"Come on, men!" shouted Origer taking up his blade and running out the door.

"Fire!" shouted Clut. FOOSH, the walls rained with arrows plummeting down on the Vikings, crushing their numbers and slowly their momentum giving Origer time to...

"Attack!" he shouted.

The men ran like the wind in to battle, slicing, cutting, chopping, mincing, mashing, crushing, crunching, splitting and killing the Vikings. Oring made his way around to the catapults. For more and more Vikings poured from the forest and soon Origer's knights would be over whelmed.

"Ready?" asked Oring to the catapult men.

"Yes, sir", said the catapult captain.

"Then send them all to hell!" shouted Oring.

"Fire", shouted the catapult captain. Ropes were cut and blocks were moved as catapult after catapult launched large chunks of rock in to the air to come and bowl down the Vikings.

They launched rock after rock smashing down in to the lines of Vikings. They lit bags of oil, loaded and fired, they hit the ground and exploded in to a wave of fire burning all in range.

After crushing and slicing Vikings left and right and centre they punched large numbers in to their lines, which caused them to retreat.

"They are retreating!" shouted a knight.

"Back inside!" shouted Origer.

The knights ran back inside Vocar and the doors were locked and bolted, archers on the wall standing ready for another assault. Knights held large planks of wood on the doors and catapults were loaded, the captain awaiting orders.

The battle field was quiet.

The court was up and the king's and queen, with one prince were in meeting.

"Now, we have this straight, people, Gergriff now has an army and four of the five stone's", said Origer.

"That is correct", said Clut.

"Then what is to be done?" asked Oring.

There was silence throughout the room as they looked at each other.

"War", said Origer quietly.

"What?" asked Claw.

"They attacked us, we must hit back, hard", said Origer.

"The Wastes are a dangerous place. To move an army would be impossible", said Claw.

"There's one way", said Clut.

"Yes?" asked Oring.

"There was one man who escaped that dark tower. He knows the way in he could lead an army in", said Clut.

"Where is this man?" asked Oring. "Mount Moon, but I've no idea where in the mountain, but there is one clue that he left, he said only in time would he be needed – *Under the hill next to the mirror the sun will show for the mountain of the north third to the top he will lie*", Clut translated from a small scroll.

"What kind of clue is that?" said Origer.

"A hard one", said Clut.

"We'll never find him with that", said Claw.

"We could", said Clut.

"Even if we did find this man, who would go?" asked Claw.

The room once again fell silent as Origer then blurted out, "I will go".

The room gasped and was in shock.

"No", said Oring.

"Why not?" asked Origer.

"It will be too dangerous", said Oring.

"What's life without danger?" said Origer.

"Longer", laughed Beakey, everyone turned to him not laughing at his joke.

"Sorry", said Beakey, being pushed back down in to his place.

"You can't go, you're my son, future king", said Oring.

"I can't just stay here, those Vikings will be back and we'll beat them back, but they will be back again with Gergriff's full army, they'll take us out, one by one until the city falls", said Origer.

"This city will never fall, but I will, you need to be king", said Oring.

"If I'm going to be king someday, then I need to do great things, like winning this war and returning peace", said Origer.

Oring then fell silent for he knew he would lose this argument.

"Then you will go", said Clut.

It looked like things were sorted but then a ninja ran in to the room puffing and panting.

"Claw… Claw", puffed the ninja.

"What is it, man?" asked Claw.

"You better come see", said the ninja.

The ninja led the kings and queen with the others out to the wall looking over the plains.

"Look", said the ninja pointing out in to the trees where they saw the Vikings. They had built a camp, lots of tents and fires around the castle cutting them off from the world.

"That could be a problem", said Claw.

"We're cut off. How will we get out?" asked Origer.

"How many horses do you have?" asked Clut.

"A couple hundred, but why?" asked Oring.

"Time for a charge then; a run will get you through. They won't be able to chase you and keep guard on us", said Clut.

"Right, prep the horses", said Oring.

Again for the third time that night, the warning bell filled the castle with sound, as the knights set the horses ready for a charge. In Origer's room Beakey made him ready to leave, not in armour but dressed as a peasant. His father walked in holding a handful of weapons.

"I know that this was not the night you wanted", said Oring.

"It's OK, Father", said Origer.

"You will have one chance to do this", said Oring.

"I know, just make sure the castle is still standing when I come back", said Origer.

"Just bring yourself back, son", said Oring hugging his son. Then standing back and giving him a sword.

"This is the sword of my great grandfather. It was used in The Stone War (the same sword that was used on the Last Day) and now it is yours, it will lead you to victory", said Oring passing him a long silver sword with a golden handle filled with patterns and symbols. At the bottom was a red gem.

"Thank you", said Origer.

"And you, Beakey, this is for you", said Oring passing a bow and a quiver of arrows to him.

"What's this?" asked Beakey.

"It belonged to my mother", said Oring.

"Why are you giving it to me?" asked Beakey.

"You are to protect my son, with your life", said Oring.

"Yes, sir", said Beakey.

"Beakey go to, make yourself ready", said Origer.

"Yes, sir", said Beakey walking out of the room leaving the king and his son to talk.

Beakey went back to his house, where he got ready. He opened the door and walked out. He had long brown trousers, a belt with a simple old sword, and a long black raincoat with a large green hood. On his back was the King's mother's quiver and bow and on his head was his old pirate hat. Massive the hat was, large and blue. He started to walk to the courtyard where the horses were being made ready when he ran in to Sandy.

"Are you going?" asked Sandy.

"Yes", said Beakey.

"Please take this for good luck", said Sandy giving him a white scarf.

"I will, thank you", said Beakey, as he put it around his neck, tied a knot and put it down in to his coat.

"Come back", said Sandy.

"I will, just be here when I do", said Beakey.

Sandy looked down.

"Goodbye", said Beakey, as he started to turn, but Sandy grabbed his coat and pulled him in to a kiss before he could leave.

Chapter 3
The Quest Begins

As the sun started to come above the hill that hid the light, the large gates of Vocar opened. The horse stood just behind the gates; Origer on the front horse with Beakey behind him in the second roll.

"Head for the river on the other side of this forest it should be far enough to escape the Vikings reach", said Oring. He looked up at his son sitting on the horse.

"Yes, Father", said Origer.

"Good luck", said Oring.

Origer walked forward with Beakey on his left and Glyn on his right.

He slowly started to walk out of the castle on the horse; he stopped halfway down the stone path. There was line after line of horses walking down after him. As Origer reached the bottom of the path the Vikings were on alert as they were grabbing weapons, pulling people out of tents and getting ready to fight.

Origer once again stopped. He slowly drew his glorious sword and held it up in front of him.

"Horsemen of Vocar we have one mission: to pass the Viking lines and reach Mount Moon. War has been declared on the Wastes and on the mountain is information needed to win the war. You are the knights for this quest. We fight and we win, let the battle begin!" shouted Origer. He cracked the horse reins as he charged to the forest. Beakey charged with his bow ready and Glyn charged with a mouth of sharp teeth. The cavalry lined up in mass, as the knights drew their swords and pointed their spears. Horns were blown as the massive band of horsemen began to charge

The horses ran out of the castle and charged; as they left the gates were locked up.

"Fire!" shouted Stron the leader of the Vikings.

Stron stood very tall. He had a cloak made from the skin of a bear. His chest was covered in armour. His muscles were breaking his straps around his arms. On his head was a wooden helmet with two horns sticking out. The Vikings cheered and cried as they ran. The order to fire was given, and the Viking launched large chunks of rocks in to the air smashing into the field crushing few horses. Other Vikings threw axes at the incoming horses. Origer had the advantage as soon as his horse entered the woods. They chopped down Viking after Viking. The catapults were crushed, tents were broken and the horses continued their way through the forest but a large number of Vikings pulled up a rope and tripped up lines of men until Glyn jumped at the rope and cut it with his teeth. He then turned and jumped at a Viking, ripping off his hands.

"Come on!" shouted Origer.

They continued deeper in to the woods, but traps had been set, ropes were cut and trees fell blocking paths, knocking off heads, crushing horses and slowing Origer's momentum.

"Move", said Origer. Guiding his horse to another path, he looked around to see few men following him. For the rest were being cut down, without mercy, killed like vermin. Origer turned to look the other way where he saw Stron, thinking to himself that he would kill the leader. Origer immediately changed course and charged straight at him followed by Glyn.

"Get him, boy", said Origer.

Glyn jumped at Stron, but he knocked the wolf flying.

"Bring it on", said Origer, whipping his reins and charging in.

"Origer stop!" shouted Beakey.

Stron saw Origer and he stood ready. Origer's horse got closer and closer. He took his feet from the stirrups and he jumped at Stron swinging his sword. But in the split second before landing the blow Stron took the swing and smashed Origer back in to a tree. Origer jumped up and went again to kill but he was pulled away by Beakey, heaving him on to the back of his horse.

"What are you doing?" asked Origer.

"My job. It won't be good if you died on day one", said Beakey riding them away from the battle followed by Glyn.

"Men, this way!" shouted Origer holding his sword in the air as Beakey led them deeper and deeper in to the forest.

Oring looked from the castle in to the battle that he could see. "God's speed, son, God's speed", he said.

Claw and Clut came up behind him. He turned. "Finish it", he said.

"Fire!" shouted Clut.

The walls lined with archers launched arrow's, flying high in to the air to shower down on the forest. But the rain of pain hardly damaged the Vikings for the cover of trees protected most of them.

Far from the castle now the horses that were left made their way from the forest, charging all the way to the White River. The number of men had cut down from 200 to 11. They waited by the river. They found a small cove hidden behind large rocks with only one way in.

"What now?" asked Beakey. He sat down and started to pet Glyn.

"Make camp. We wait to see if any more come", said Origer.

"Yes, sir", said one of the soldiers, who went by the name of Blike

They roped the horses, to the close trees and they built a small fire in the centre of the rocks and a pot of stew was put on.

"You two pull that rock over here", said Origer pointing to a large flat rock.

Two of the knights pushed the flat rock across to Origer.

"Right men come round", said Origer opening a large map over the rock.

"So we are here by this river", said Origer pointing. "Then we're heading here and then here, Mount Moon." He pointed to a mountain range then pulled his finger across the page to the Wastes.

"How long will it take?" asked Beakey.

"The fastest way would be a two day ride to here, the forbidden forest. That forest will be the fastest way instead of taking a 600 mile detour", said Blike.

"What's the supply count?" asked Origer.

"We have enough for all of us for about two to three days. Not much made it through the Viking lines", said a knight.

"We could stop here", said another knight pointing to a small village, on the map.

"So the plan: head here to re-supply, then track through the forest, find the mountain and save the world" said Origer. "Who is with me?" he asked putting his sword on the rock.

There was much suspense until Beakey placed his sword on the rock.

Then each and everyone of the other knights took their swords and put them on the rock. Even Glyn put his paw on to the rock.

"Help!" shouted a voice from beyond the rocks.

"What's that?" asked Origer.

They walked out of the cover of the rocks to see a wounded man pulling another half dead man on a horse. He was covered in damaged, torn armour and dripping in blood.

"Get him in", said Origer.

They ran out and helped to pull them behind cover. They got the man off the horse and started to patch him up with water from the river and supplies from one of the bags. They were lucky that one of the men with them was a doctor, Dr Rick.

"How is he, doc?" asked Origer.

"He'll be fine with rest", said Rick.

He patched the man up the best he could and they kept him lying next to the fire to keep warm.

A couple of men started to rest, while others were on guard looking over the field for threats and dangers.

The day went on and the night came up, the field went dark and the knight's made the fire bigger. But as they slept they were unaware that eyes were watching and waiting until the morning came.

The sun slowly started to rise on that misty morning. The land was filled with a thick mist as the knight started to pack up their stuff and tie it to the horse.

"It's early", said one of the knights.

"Yes", yawned Beakey.

"We have to get a move on, we've been here too long", said Origer.

They packed the packs, stuffed the stuff and filled the funnels. They were almost ready to go until it they heard the snap of a stick. The knights looked up into the mist as it fell silent. Origer drew his sword and started to back up as the knights did the same, each one took up an arm and they stood all back to back in a circle looking around into the mist.

"What is it?" asked Beakey quietly.

"Something's out there", said Origer looking closer in to the mist. Then came the sound of SPLASH!.

"It's in the water", said Origer. The circle walked away from the water's edge.

"Who's there?, Show yourself!" shouted Origer.

"GARD GARD MARG", said a voice.

"Uh oh", said Origer.

"What is it?" asked Beakey.

"Water lore men", said Origer.

"What's that?" asked Beakey.

"That", said Origer pointing to a figure walking out of the river.

"Looks normal", said Beakey.

But as it got closer, It looked less human and turned more fishy. A hideous creature emerged from the mist, the head of a frog, fin hands and legs. A body covered in loads of different colours.

"Good God", said one of the knights.

Beakey took out an arrow and pointed it at the lore man.

"One we can handle", said Beakey. Glyn growled in agreement and got ready to jump.

But no one else agreed for they saw more and more lore men coming out of the water.

"Everyone, we going to quickly run to the horses, ready?" asked Origer. "Go!" he shouted. The group split and Beakey let the arrow fly right in to the lore man's face. Glyn jumped at another and tore at its throat. They ran screaming and gurgling as the battle began. One came up to Blike. He answered with a large punch across the face knocking him right into another knight's sword. Each knight battled and tried to get on to their horses but in the process of getting on the horse the lore men would pull them off and kill them.

"Come on", said Origer. Now on his horse, he sent his sword down a lore man's throat.

"Eat that", said Beakey, putting an arrow in another's mouth.

He jumped on to his horse and whipped the reins.

The horses made their way away from the large rocks. Glyn jumped up after and ran with Origer his mouth full of green blood. They started to charge across the field. But as they charged, the sad truth was that there were only five of them left: Origer, Beakey, Blike, Rick and the wounded knight. Origer turned and was shocked.

"Where... where's the rest" he asked.

"Gone", said Beakey.

"Not again?" said Origer. "Come on, move", he said smashing the reins down, doubling the horse's speed.

After a close call and a skipped meal they spent the day charging across the plains of Thringer. On their way they passed many inspiring things. The first thing they passed was the endless bog. A land full of sludge, leading forever, nought but the colour of brown and green. Many a people have lost their way through this bog, because of its fog. It bends the mind causing you to go in circles. It was lucky that the heroes were on horseback, animals are not tricked but this mist; they ran through safely.

Another thing to come in their path was the orange wall. A large earthquake once hit Thringer which caused a land push. A massive chunk of land was pushed from the ground forming the orange wall. It got the name of orange because the stone that was pushed up was an old orange stone that was unnatural to come from these lands. The orange wall splits the land beautifully. It created a good border for the kingdom of men. So as they passed the wall, they were officially across the border.

And another on our tour is the White River. A river filled with rocks with the shape to make water frothy and white, so the name. It travel from one side of the world to the other.

They came to a stone built bridge crossing the White River.

"Look", said Origer pointing.

They were over the bridge and the village was in sight, still far away but close enough to get there by night.

"Come on, we're almost there", said Origer, now with Glyn sleeping on his lap. He started up his horse again as they slowed their speed on their way to the village.

It started again to get darker, but the village got closer, so as soon as the sun set, the five horses slowly walked into the village.

It was a small village but hard working. There were many wooden houses and bars. There were hand carts, horse stables, haystacks, food supplies, pig pens and large tall poles with massive fire burning at the top of each of them lighting the town.

Origer led his men up to one of the inns called The Blue Sky .

They roped the horses outside then took their stuff off the saddles and they went inside the bar.

The door opened and their noses were filled with the warm smell of ale and tobacco. Inside there was a massive warm fire burning in the corner. There was a long smooth bar covered in old glasses, spilt drink and drunken men. There were massive barrels stacked up behind the bar filled with all kinds of drink. They walked towards the bar, where a barmaid was sitting reading a book. She looked up and then stood.

"Evening, gents", said the barmaid.

"Evening", said Origer.

"What can I get for you?" asked the maid, winking.

"We need rooms for the night?" said Origer.

"Oh I say, can do", she said, and she put her hand under the bar and pulled out a set of keys.

"Eight gold pieces?" asked the maid opening her other hand for Origer to drop the coins in. He took the coins out of his bag and put them in her hand one by one.

"My room down the hall", said the maid pulling Origer closer and whispering in his ear.

"Thank you", said Origer, taking the key and moving up the stairs quickly, because the maid watched as he ran.

"Do you know her?" asked Beakey.

"No" said Origer, unlocking the door.

"OK, well goodnight", said Beakey leaving the room.

The others came in and chose their bed. Glyn chose to sleep on Origer.

Chapter 4

The Weapon Of Dark Matter

Our scene will now change from a small village to the dark lands of the Wastes. A dark and cold place filled with dark purple sand with dark gasping wind that would kill. A fortress with a tower and a mess of a village for the servants of evil, sat at the middle of the Wastes.

The Wastes on their own are surrounded by large un-climbable mountains except for the Valley of Skulls. A very dangerous way to travel, if you don't know the path that is. It is the only way into the Wastes.

But to the tower; very tall. Very, very tall. Over twenty floors of terror. The outside covered in bones and fires; lots of odd shaped things pointing off it. Odd shaped windows and a very strange door. At the top of a set of stairs were two large black doors, with massive golden handles; the type of door a giant would have. The lock was small, and had many gears and cogs splitting off it connecting a large pole that held the door closed and locked. Behind those doors was the bottom floor of the tower, a simple empty room with nothing but a spiral staircase. At the back of the room leading up through the tower. The next two floors were armouries, where weapons where kept for battles. Many axes and sword's, arrows and knifes not made of steel but made from stone, bone, wood and rope. They were bad, but still good enough to do the job of killing. Four floors later were filled with papers and books, ink and quills. The full history of Gergriff life was in those rooms. As were spells and magic.

Two floors later you passed through the kitchen and food store. Even an immortal man has to eat. Another set of four floors were filled with pots and cauldrons, all types of plants and herbs used to make bombs and deadly poison. Bottles of coloured water with all types of magic properties and useful content.

The next floor had Gergriff's throne, a large black chair as tall as the room covered in spikes and weird decoration. In the centre of the room sat a large altar with a giant crystal ball. Unknown is how they work. Even I don't know so I have to skip. The next five floors… well Gergriff had filled these two rooms with his treasures. There were large stashes and weird paintings, all his golden trophies, his enemies' heads, old weapons, all kinds of trinkets and his own mother's and father's ashes, sitting in two large vases sitting on another two large altars.

Now that we've been through that, we come to the last floor, where Gergriff was standing in the middle of another four altars, each with a part of the great stone. The room itself was completely black nothing on the walls, no windows, no painting, no pots or papers.

Gergriff stood in the centre of the room; he was wearing a very long robe, a black belt with a large deadly sword, the handle shaped like a dragon with two jewels for eyes. He looked young for an old man.

"Master", said Gergriff looking up, his eyes filled with an evil glare.

The room was empty, until the door locked itself and black smoke started to form a black ball. The room grew cold and an evil presence started to form. The ball started to float up, in the centre of the room. As it began to speak it glowed white with yellow and purple flashing on every word.

"What?" asked Master. As it talked it was the voice of hell, the deep dark voice came from the twisted evil throat of the devil himself.

"Master, I have the four stones", said Gergriff.

"Four! Where is the fifth?" shouted Master, easily angered.

"In Vocar", said Gergriff getting on to his knees.

"We need the fifth or my plan will never prevail", said Master.

"The plan is working, it is only a matter of time till we have it. But I need help. The walls of Vocar are not so easily broken and I have not but goblins", said Gergriff.

"For my plan to work I will give you three gifts", said Master.

"Thank you, Master", said Gergriff.

"The gifts that I will give will win the war. The first that I give to you are the seeds of Gironlyor", said Master.

As he said it smoke broke away from the ball and materialised into a small bag, as Gergriff took them.

"Next is the vial of Rockcorly", said Master.

Again another cloud came away and turned into a bottle, no bigger than a bottle of wine filled with pink liquid.

"Last I give to you the elemental weapon of dark matter. This is no normal weapon, this is only for the sons of hell. No mortal can use this weapon. Now it is your turn to wield her", said Master.

This time instead of a pot or a bottle. The cloud slowly filled the room with black matter. As it started to spin around and around Gergriff, the wind got faster and faster. Gold specks of light floated off the spinning matter, the light came together in the shape of a scythe, weapon of the dead. The light slowly started to form together until the weapon imploded and turned from gold to black. It stretched back out and formed a scythe; it floated slowly into the air. Gergriff slowly put out his hand and put it on the weapon as soon. As his skin made contact the dark power filled him as he fell to his knees over flowing with evil. Everything stopped and Gergriff was left there kneeling. Staring up taking in all of what was happening.

"I leave it to you, my servant of evil", said Master as the black cloud disappeared in to thin air.

"Thank you, Master", said Gergriff. He stood and looked at his new weapon.

Now that he had the gifts, it was time to use them. He made his way down and out of his tower. He walked away from the tower to a large flat piece of rocky land. He took out the vile of Rockcorly, he pulled out the cork and dipped the water all over the rocks leaving half for later. He put the cork back in and walked back from the wet rocks.

"Come to me", said Gergriff. Pulling his weapon out of a black cloud of smoke. He gave it a spin and stabbed it into the floor, it fell silent until, CRACK. The rocks started to split and break, as the floor rumbled and rocks were pushed out of the ground. More and more rocks were pushed from the land as they started to form into the shape of giant people.

"You will follow me", said Gergriff holding his weapon up above them.

The face of the rocks started to glow with a mouth and nose all burning as the colour of yellow.

The giant rocks looked at him until the front monster bowed and said, "Leader",

"Leader", said the rest as they bowed.

"Great", said Gergriff. "With me", he said walking away.

He made his way back to the tower when a goblin came up to him. A goblin dressed in rags, a rope belt with a bone knife and the skin colour of green, a horrible sight to see.

"What is this, sir?" asked Slime, looking at the rock giants.

"These are our reinforcements, give them weapons and send them to aid the Vikings", said Gergriff.

"Yes, sir", said Slime.

Gergriff walked out from the other side of the tower. This time with several goblins, he walked to another flat plain.

"What are we doing?" asked Slime.

"Shut up", said Gergriff lifting the bag. He used his magic and the seeds floated away and fell out on to the ground and again it fell silent.

"That's it?" asked Slime.

"That man will be killed if he does not shut up", said Gergriff, pointing his weapon at Slime's throat.

Then CRACK! The floor, once again started to crack and from the floor grew not rock's but vines; large green vines splitting out of the ground, tying together, roping together, growing higher and higher up into the air. It grew and grew until it started to pass up through the clouds. It was growing until it suddenly stopped for it had grown enough to get where it was going.

"Move", said Gergriff. He smashed his weapon on the ground and he then turned into a cloud of darkness much like his master, he then started to float up the plant.

"Come on!" shouted cloud Gergriff. The goblins started to jump and climb up the plant.

They climbed and climbed, the four of them passed up through the cloud to be shocked at what they saw. For what they saw was a giant chunk of floating rock, with the plant smashing up into the bottom.

They made their way up inside of the rock, mouths hanging open, panting and looking at what they saw. The walls were coated in an orange jelly-like material. There was a set of stairs leading up through the rock.

"Success", said Gergriff pointing his weapon out.

They split at the vine and looked around inside the rock until, "Sir!" shouted Trog.

Gergriff and the other goblins made it over to where Trog had found a very large hand hanging out of the jelly wall. This was no normal hand, and besides it large size, the hand itself was covered in mould, large untrimmed nails and many wounds.

Gergriff stood back and pointed his hand. He closed his eyes and pulled his hand. The giant hand started to be pulled from the jelly wall, it was pulled and pulled until it started to move out. The arm got long as a large shadow started to appear on the other side of jelly and then SPLIT, the jelly gave and a giant fell out of the wall smashing down on the floor.

The Giant, a massive creature, covered still in green mould wearing clothes, held a very large wooden club. The face more ugly than a goblin (but don't let him hear you say it), large dripping nose, doll stupid eyes, and dripping ears, rotting hair and a rusty helmet.

"Oy", said Gergriff smacking its face with his weapon. The giant groaned and moved. Gergriff smacked it again and it started to wake.

"Where, where is I?" said the giant pulling itself to his feet.

"Oy", said Gergriff.

"What, no time, must win stone war", said the giant slowly moving itself across the ground.

"Giant?" asked Gergriff.

"What?" asked Giant.

"Your name?" asked Gergriff.

"Grown", said Grown.

"Grown, the stone war is over. You lost", said Gergriff.

"What?... what!" shouted Grown. He picked up his mallet and started smashing it around.

"Oy, we have another chance", said Gergriff.

"Yes", said Grown as he stopped his range and bent down to Gergriff.

"We win?" asked Grown.

"We will but I need your alliance", said Gergriff.

"My alliance you have", said Grown tilting his head.

"Great", said Gergriff. He smashed his staff on the floor and filled the inside of the stone with black lightning. Bolts shot everywhere burning the jelly to dust as giants again and again fell out of the walls smashing to the ground. They picked up large clumsy weapons and with very long and dozy expressions they looked to their leader.

"The war is on, we fight and win. To war!" shouted Grown.

The giants started to "cheer" as they all waved their weapons up and down in the air.

"To war!" shouted Gergriff. He closed into the cloud and started to fly out of the rock and back down the plant. As the Giants cheered and ran and jumped out of the hole like mad men, they fell and grabbed to the out-hanging branches. They dropped from branch to branch until they hit the floor.

So after they all grabbed weapons and prepared armour, Gergriff walked out of his tower. Standing on the top of his stairs looking down on his army; Goblins, rock monsters and giants.

"We once lost this land, we were beaten down like dogs. Now we will rule as kings. The land is ours, let us take it back!" shouted Gergriff raising his weapon, shooting lightning bolts in to the sky.

"To war!" shouted Grown.

The armies, cheering and screaming, started to run to battle. They quickly started making their way from the Wastes with Gergriff riding a black horse. Leading the lines of evil creatures, line after line, squad after squad, an army of 50000 evil creatures marched over the Wastes heading to war.

Chapter 5
The Bar

It was morning and Origer was hanging out of his bed, feet in the air, face on the ground. He yawned and opened his eyes and was very shocked to see an arrow just inches from stabbing him in the head.

"That could have been messy", said Origer, moving the arrow away, pushing it back under Beakey's bed.

Origer got up to see the mess the room was in; the other five beds all in a mess with each person hanging out on every side and Glyn lying over Beakey, who had come in at some point in the night.

"Everyone up!" shouted Origer.

Suddenly the room jumped as they all woke up in a panic

"Where is he?, Where is he?" said Blike, jumping up with a sword holding it under Origer's throat.

"Oh it's you", said Blike, taking the sword away.

"Everyone up", said Origer.

"Yes?" asked Blike.

"The quest must move, no time for sleeping. Vocar is waiting", said Origer.

"Can't we have a drink first?" asked Beakey.

"Only one", said Origer.

"Sir, we going to stay here", said Rick.

"What?" asked Origer.

"We're just going to slow you down", said Rick.

"OK, good luck", said Origer shaking his hand.

"Till we meet again", said Rick.

So they packed up their stuff and made their way to the bar all dressed up in their large warm coats. Sacks on their backs, they dropped them and sat at the bar.

"Three", said Origer.

"Sure thing, lads", said the maid. She picked up three glasses and put them under the barrel tap. Origer noticed that as she filled the jugs her hand was shaking.

He decided to ignore it, the INN that morning had only four others in; two over by the fire and two the other side of the room, all dressed in long black coats with heads down.

Origer didn't start to get suspicious until two more men dressed in long black coats and capes, sat down at the other end of the bar.

"I think we are in trouble", whispered Origer.

"What?" asked Beakey whispering back.

"Look around", whispered Origer.

Beakey stretched and pretending to stretch his back, he turned to look.

"Full of men", whispered Beakey turning back around.

"Let's go then", said Origer.

"Here you go, boys", said Lin putting the glasses on the table.

"Drink first", said Beakey, who was gulping down the ale.

"But…" said Origer. As he started to move the door opened and three more men dressed the same walked in.

"Forget it", said Origer. He stood up and turned around to the bar, full of people.

"Before we get started, do any of you want to leave?" asked Origer.

It fell quiet, before tables were pushed and smashed over, as all of the guys stood holding up weapons, looking at Origer.

"Come easy and be killed", said Jack. One of the men bigger than the rest, he stood in the centre of his gang, and he held an overly large axe.

Blike and Origer were both standing ready for a fight, but Beakey was still drinking until he said "Come and be killed. I would hate to hear option number two", said Beakey still sitting.

"How did you know we're here?" asked Origer

"Viking are very quick with bounties", said Jack.

"I see", said Origer.

Jack looked at Beakey sitting.

"Stand up, boy", said Jack.

"OK" said Beakey. He stood, put down his glass and spun around. In a split second he drew and shot an arrow across the bar right in to

Jack's chest, ripping through his armour, stuck. Jack looked at it, then he pulled it out and gave Beakey a dirty look.

"Oh, that's not fair", said Beakey.

"Kill them", said Jack. On his command, the other men jumped in to attack. Blike sliced on one, then defended against two others.

Origer stabbed, punched and kicked as he defended against the last. Beakey looked at Jack and Jack looked at Beakey.

"Let's roll", said Beakey. He dropped his bow, grabbed a bar stool and smashed it over Jack's head, Jack fell back, as he then grabbed Beakey and launched him across the room to smash in the back of the bar. Beakey hit a barrel and fell to the floor. The barrel cracked and filled Beakey's mouth with ale.

But he had to fight, so he pulled himself up to the bar only to duck from Jack's fist which flowed across, hitting and getting stuck in to one of the barrels and ale sprayed everywhere. Beakey then had an idea, Jack's hand was stuck in a barrel, so Beakey stood to his full height' and broke the tap of the barrel above Jack and SPLASH, ale went everywhere pushing Jack on to the floor.

Jack got to his feet, eyes red from the ale. He swung his axe and whacked Beakey across the bar. Beakey hit the wall and lay on the floor, again half out, half in; he couldn't hear, or see well. Jack walked up to him but Beakey pulled his strength to try and pull his sword out of its scabbard, but no luck.

Jack came to him. He put his axe up in to the air and was about to bring it down on Beakey before, SLICE, a sword came out of Jack's chest from the other side. Jack tried to move; he grabbed the sword but then fell flat on his face. Origer stood behind him with a blood covered sword.

"Beakey?" asked Origer.

Beakey turned his head as he started to see and hear again. He was pulled to his feet by Origer but still dizzy.

"Ow", said Beakey, holding his head.

"What's wrong?" asked Blike.

"Too much ale", said Beakey laughing. Origer and Blike, looked at each other then back to Beakey who had fallen down again.

"Time to go", said Origer.

"Right", said Beakey.

The three of them left the bar, and walked up to their horse.

"Right, Blike, find us a cart. Beakey you visit the blacksmith, and I'll take a trip to the market. Meet back at this bar as fast as you can. We're not safe here. But we need supplies so move!" shouted Origer.

They split and went throughout the village; Blike to a house which had a covered workshop where an old village man was cutting wood.

"Sir?" asked Blike.

"Ay, what's that, Sonny?" asked the old man.

"Need a cart?" asked Blike.

"No my name's not Bart", said the old man, not having the best hearing.

"No, carts, I said carts", said Blike.

"I have no time for darts, I have to finish this cart", said the old man getting back to his work.

Blike slapped his face in his hand and huffed, "hurr" he went.

Beakey walked up to a large blacksmith. A massive covered smiths with a large fire, a large metal work bench and weapons hanging off the walls.

"Impressive", said Beakey.

"What, Sonny?" asked an old man that was very similar looking to the old man at the cart store.

"Yes well I need some new weapons?" asked Beakey.

The blacksmith walked away and came back holding an axe.

"Not them. Swords", said Beakey.

"Got ya", said the old man. He walked off and came back with arrows and bows.

"No. Swords", said Beakey.

The old man walked off again and yet again came back with a spear.

"Oh", said Beakey, slapping his face, into his hand and huffing.

Let's go to see Origer. He was having better luck; he had a sack of carrots, a bag of potatoes, stacks of bread all in a very large sack. He walked up to a store which sold cheeses. Origer tapped the desk.

"Hello?" asked Origer.

A man turned around from his cutting table and the man was old. He looked the same as the other two men that day.

"Cheese", said Origer.

"Right", said the old man, holding up a bowl of peas.

"Not peas, cheese", said Origer.

"OK, I see", said the old man. He put the peas back and he dived under the table to bring up a set of keys.

"Oh", said Origer slapping his face into his hand.

So the three met back as quick as they could. They put the things they got into the cart. Beakey finally got weapons and Origer finally got the chesses.

So Origer led Blike while Beakey led a horse that pulled the cart. As they moved out of the village they started to cross land with speed but not too fast for the cart contents would fly everywhere.

Chapter 6
The Forbidden forest

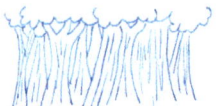

They travelled the days and rested the nights but for the next, they were looking up at the Forbidden Forest. The name explains it all. 'Forbidden Forest.' They looked up at the black wood. The trees were rotten and filled with poison, no light was able to break through into the forest itself. To look into the forest would be like to look at the night; trees up to 60 meters tall, but still black as night.

"Do we?" asked Blike.

"Yes, we don't have the time", said Origer.

"Hold on", said Beakey. They both looked around to see Beakey trying to hold the horse. But the horse was going mad at the sight of the forest. He battled and Beakey pulled until SNAP, the reins broke and the horses bolted. It ran and broke off the cart and the supplies were thrown over the ground.

Glyn was fine he wasn't spooked by the forest.

"Oops", said Beakey falling to the floor.

"Leave them", said Origer.

"Pick up the gear, we are going in on foot", said Origer.

"Can't we go around?" asked Beakey. He walked up to the broken cart, and started to pick up the stuff.

"Beakey, hundreds of miles on foot, we wouldn't be able to do it on horse", explained Origer.

"Blike", said Origer, throwing him a sword. Blike caught it and strapped it to his belt.

Beakey strapped up a large sack and put it over his shoulder. Then he threw Blike a bag of pots and pans, but not being ready to catch, he dropped them with a clang. Beakey shoved the rest into another massive sack and carried it along.

"You dozy prawn", said Blike.

"Are you coming?" said Origer.

He slowly started to walk in to the forest. As they went in deeper the poisoned overgrowth got thicker and darker. Walking through an old path made of cobble all mangled by the roots of the plants and trees, breaking the path causing them to walk in circles.

"Keep to the path", said Origer.

"Yes, sir", said Blike.

"Beakey?" asked Origer. Turning around to see Beakey, he was trying to pull one of the bags that was caught in a tree.

"It's stuck", said Beakey.

"I can see that. Pull it", said Origer.

"I'm trying", said Beakey. He pulled at the strap, he put one foot up on the tree, then the other, so soon his whole body weight was being held up by a branch.

"Stand back", said Blike and he took out a new sword. He held it high and brought it down on to the plant with force. SNAP the plant broke, but the sword was now bent.

"Look at that", said Blike, pointing to the sword.

"It's bent", said Beakey looking up from the floor. For he had dropped from a tree.

"Come on", said Origer.

They spent hours, or days, unknown the time. They made their way through the forest always keeping to the path. For being in the forest, so long, they had quite forgotten what sunlight was, so they stopped when they were tired and moved when they could. As they moved, the forest just got thicker and thicker. The forest was silent as a cemetery. Silent no animals, no rabbits, moles, ferrets, no birds, no squirrels and no people as yet until one night or well they thought it was night. Like I said it was hard to tell when it was night.

They found a large tree with roots pushed out of the ground causing a small wooden cave to form, so they decide to set up camp.

"How's it coming?" asked Blike.

"Almost done", said Beakey looking in to the pot.

"Where?" said Blike looking at Origer's map.

"I must've been over it five times. We started here we should have got to the other side by now", said Origer.

"Maybe we're lost", said Blike.
"We can't be, we're following the path", said Origer.

So the night went on, they ate and again went to the map. But as the fire went out they dozed off.

"Z Z Z Z", they went off into the night.

But as they slept creatures started to emerge from the bushes and trees. Creatures abnormal; nothing like a creature of earth. They were a mess to describe them, simply, they looked like a blue skinned goblin. But a lot more disgusting. They may not be of this earth but they still have a name. The creature is called a Trec, not a normal name, but it's not a normal creature.

They walked in to the small camp, very silent on their feet and started to look around their things. They took the food, the spuds, carrots and cheese, more of the Trec's went into Origer's things and took the gold coins. One walked up to Beakey and slowly pulled the sword from Beakey's hand, for he was holding his sword close.

But their luck expired when one of the Trec's pulled at the bag of pots and a pan fell and CLANG, it hit the ground. Origer shot up to see a Trec going through his pockets.

"Ah!" he shouted, kicking the Trec across the camp.

"Up!" shouted Origer, pulling up his spear and throwing it. He then grabbed his sword from the fire. The point was red hot and made a very painful mark on the enemy.

"What?" said Beakey, looking up to see a Trec. He punched the Trec taking his sword. Then getting to his feet drawing a sword, the three got up all back to back kicking, punching and slicing the Trec's.

Glyn was up and he jumped up and tore off the Trec's face.

"Too many", said Blike.

"No it's not", said Beakey. He grabbed the large pan from the fire and smashed it over a Trec's head, then kicking the next. When Blike took two Trec's head's off. Origer kicked one and stabbed another, but the more they killed the more attacked. Until they stopped when lines and lines of spears were pointing at them.

"Ah", said Blike pushing a point from his noise.

"What do you want?" asked Origer. Looking at the creature. The creatures, not knowing how to speak English, picked up long tubes and shot sleeping darts at them. It went dark and quiet as they each fell to the floor.

"Sleepy time", said Beakey as he fell in to a deep snore.

Being knocked out opened Origer's mind to memory, he was standing in a dark room when he heard a devilish voice.

"Hello, Origer", said the voice.

"What? Who's there?" said Origer drawing his sword.

No answer, just an evil laugh which turned the blood cold, but the dream was over as Origer fell back into this world.

He opened his eyes to see darkness, his eyes slowly adjusted and he started to see much better. But only to see that the Trec had him roped by hands and legs to a pole and he was being carried through the forest. Even Glyn was roped up. The Trec's were walking through their tree home, a very large series of wooden planks, logs and lots of ropes not built well, but built well enough to work, badly cut planks from sticks to stalks. Floors made of boxes and bundles. Again Origer turned his head back to see Beakey and Blike both also roped up swinging on poles.

"Ay- up", said Beakey. Looking at Origer.

"Where are we?" asked Origer.

"I don't know", said Beakey.

"You're coming to our leader", said one of the Trecs who spoke English.

There are only a handful of Trec's that can speak English including their leader, who we come to now.

The Trecs home lay in the centre of the forest; the largest tree in existence, so big that it broke through the leaf roof of the forest. It let in only a small amount of light, but fires were still around to keep it all lit. It was a magnificent tree but a shame that it was corrupted by the forest. The bark was black and the leaves were purple. There were mushrooms big as houses growing at its base and platforms bigger than courtyards built up with chains and ropes. Origer and the others were pulled up to a platform. In the centre sat a large throne cut into the tree it and sitting in the chair was a very short and fat Trek.

He wore a bone crown and two belts across his chest covered in heads of the people he had killed. Around his throne were boxes and bins filled with weapons. There were chests and barrels filled with gold and silver which he had taken from any passing caravans.

"Bring them here", said the leader as he dropped from his throne and walked up to the three of them. He stepped up to them and looked up at them holding his long pole covered in bones, herbs and plants and a odd thing in the top of his pole was a glass ball, with a white flower inside it.

"Who are you?" asked Origer looking down on the leader.

"I am the Trec King", said the leader, pulling Origer down so he could look him in the face.

"Why are you here?" asked the Trec king. "What this?" looking at Glyn who growled back.

"Well…" started Origer.

But Beakey kicked him in the back to stop so he could say, "King."

"What?" asked King.

"Look here you lump of blubber, you're going to let us pass or we burn this forest to the ground" said Beakey.

"Do you, sir, give us insult?" shouted King pointing his staff at Beakey. At that point the tree filled with Trec's, arrows and spears all pointing down at them.

"GULP", went Beakey.

"Now you done it", said Blike.

"You know what, human's?, You're going to die, in the most terrible ways possible", said King laughing, a very mad laugh.

He walked back to his throne. He was just about to give the order but before his hand went down an arrow shot down from the trees and landed between Origer's feet.

Everyone looked down at the arrow as it exploded in to a great bright blue light filling the tree with a glow. As the light died the Trec's looked around but Origer, Beakey, Glyn and Blike were gone.

Chapter 7
The Fight Has Started

While we leave the heroes to light up, we go to a small village, just a hundred miles from Vocar. This village did not escape to Vocar for they have their own walls and drawbridge surrounded by a moat, a fortress in itself. Tall wooden walls, built with paths for archers to defend the town. Halt, the town inside was small but made strong and a tower climbing to the tallest height had a large golden bell, which would only be sounded in the outbreak of war.

On this day the bridge was down and the farm hands were out in their fields bringing in the harvest. One of the farmers, an old man, had just bundled some of the wheat together and he heard a faint CLANG from over the hill. He stopped his work and he walked up the hill. Puffing and panting his way to the top he had a great shock when he reached the top for on the other side of the hill was an army of goblins, rock monsters and giants. The old man gulped and … next thing he knew he was running up to Halt screaming, "Attack, we under attack!".

The bell rang through Halt as the bridge and the wall filled with archers. People ran to their homes and the farmers fled from their fields and the knights and stood ready at the gate. The master of Halt walked above the gate and stood looking out to the foe.

"You creatures of the dark, you will stop!" shouted Orly.

The armies stopped, before the water and Gergriff rode up on his horse to the front.

"We will not stop", said Gergriff.

"Then we will fire", said Orly putting his hand in to the air.

"You don't have to fight. Fight and you will all die or you will go to the Wastes and only most of you will die", said Gergriff.

"Never", said Orly. He dropped his hand and the archers all launched arrows at Gergriff. In the split second of the fight Gergriff put up his hand and using his unearthly powers, the arrows stopped in mid air around him.

Gergriff smiled, he turned his hand, and the arrows still in the air turned around. Gergriff then flicked his fingers and arrows flying at twice the speed, fired back at the walls killing each and every archer.

"You still have a chance", said Gergriff.

"Launch!" said Orly. As he shouted, massive burning oil sacks launched in to the air and crushed with a fire blast.

Gergriff said no more for he turned and walked back down through his army and gave the call to attack. At the call goblins shot arrow after arrow into the walls and doors. They brought long wooden logs and they built a bridge. The giants started to pick up the goblins, as if they were going to throw stones. They threw them up over the walls on top of the knight's, the soldiers killed each one as they fell. They could easily take one by one, but as soon as one fell on to the bridge he cut the ropes and the drawbridge dropped and creatures poured in to Halt. Everyone, all the knights, all the women and children fled for their lives but they were all cut down. Halt was flooded with evil creatures, the town stood no chance. Orly fought the best he could but badly wounded he crawled his way up the tall tower where there was a great golden bell. Hanging from the bell was a long rope and Orly, using his last strength, pulled the rope and the sound of the great bell rang over miles and miles of land to the castle of Vocar.

The castle, since we were last here, had been attacked twice more by the Vikings, doing more and more damage each time. The doors were in constant rolling repair and the hospital was over filled. The kings, queen and court were in the throne room making plans of attack, when a boy burst in to the room with news from the town.

"What is it, boy?" asked Oring.

"The bell has rung from Halt", said the boy.

"Oh no. Thank you, boy, go back to your master", said Oring.

The boy left the room and the court looked back to the king.

"So, you've heard that, we are in very deep trouble, what's to be done?" asked Oring.

"Well, we have enough supplies to last another two weeks", said Clut.

"What's our solider count?" asked Claw.

"Over 18000 strong", said Oring.

"What's their numbers?" asked Claw.

"Way over 10000 Vikings and there's no idea how many more are coming. Halt is over 30 miles away so we have a little time before they give a full on attack. Gergriff is bringing his full force, so I say again how are we to escape? We can't stay here, we will never hold off an attack from Gergriff's full force", said Oring.

A great silence fell in the hall until one of the court members said, "The supply tunnel."

"What?" asked Oring.

"The tunnel that leads underground all the way to the port", he said again, but quietly.

"We can't", said Oring.

"Why not?" asked Clut.

Being much older than Claw and Clut together, he knew much about what the man was saying, so instead of himself telling them he called for an old man who was master of the library.

The doors to the room opened and a man walked in, an old man, dressed in a long, dark blue robe. In his hands he held up a large purple book. He had a very long white beard and a bald head, he wore a little blue hat and a black belt with a golden hook and a brown case for his sword (sound familiar?).

"My king", said the old man.

"Library master, I need you to read the last records of the supply tunnel", said Oring.

"My king, are you sure?" asked the old man.

"Yes", said Oring.

The old man left the room to get the book and soon returned with two knights pulling along an over-large book with a massive golden lock. It was placed down on the stairs in front of the throne. The old man pulled out a ring of keys which were hanging around his neck and he searched through the keys until he selected one to unlock the book. He pulled off the lock and read the cover.

"History records from 567 TO 577", said the old man.

The old man lifted the book to a page, he flicked a few back, then two forward, and he put his finger down the page until he stopped.

26 / 43 / 571
The mine is almost complete. The tunnel is but 30 feet from the port, with this complete we will get things into the city with great speed.

34 / 43 / 571
The mine is complete and is working as expected. To celebrate this in the castle we had a great party with supplies brought though the tunnel.

4 / 44 / 571
Two men that were bringing supplies to the castle have gone missing. Knights have been sent to search the tunnels.

53 / 44 / 571
It is a horrible time for Vocar, only today we found that the tunnel that was dug was dug through an underground nest of giant spiders. The days are growing short and the nights are long and filled with murder. Every night knights guard the tunnel and every morning they're found dead.

54 / 44 / 571
The number of spiders has tripled and they have evolved, some are now showing with arms and heads. They have started a war in the tunnel; the knights go in but never come out.

26 / 45 / 571
Battle has been raging throughout the tunnels and plans are being made. Over 200 men are sent into those tunnels.

1 / 1 / 572
A horrible day as the decision was made to seal the tunnels. The caves were closed leaving over 200 men to die at the hands of the spiders. The doors have been locked and the king has hidden the key. Those doors are never again to be opened.

"And that was the last entry of the tunnel, 35 years ago", said the old man.

"That's why we can't open them", said Oring.

"But…" said Clut.

"No buts! I sent 200 men to their deaths", shouted Oring.

"You gave 200 men so that 20000 could live. If those spiders got to the surface where would we be now?" said Claw.

"We should open it for only a short time so that we can escape", said Clut.

Oring sat in his chair and a great deal of thought ran through his head.

"Then it shall be done, prepare the bombs to blow the cave open. Make our armies ready to help the people to escape, we are leaving Vocar", said Oring.

So the orders were given and the people packed up their things and made ready to go. Bombs were made and brought in carts to the entrance of the cave where the kings and queen stood ready.

"If the spiders become a threat I will without hesitation close the caves", said Oring.

"OK", said Clut.

"Fine", said Claw.

"Right then, Claw, you will cover the cut-off tunnels while you, Clut, will guard the back and re-lock the door. I will take the front with my best knights", said Oring putting his hand out to a bunch of large, muscular men. Standing ready armed to the teeth.

"It is time", said Oring. He pulled out a string around his neck. On it was a key. He slowly put the key in to the lock.

"Stand ready", said Oring.

People moved back as the four knights stood around Oring. They put up their shields holding their swords over the top.

Oring put his hand back on the key and he slowly turned it. "CLINK." The door started to unlock. The key turned. The door clonked as it swung open.

The knights stood ready, they threw in torches to light the cave as Oring walked down a very old small set of wood stairs. The cave filled with a smell that left a bad taste in the mouth. There was a rocky tunnel with handrails and burnt out torches. Oring took ten steps closely followed by knights until he stopped at a stone wall which he had made many years ago. To keep the cave double locked.

"It's still locked", said Oring. He placed his hand on the rock and dropped his head as he could remember the many screams which came from this cave.

"Blow it open", said Oring turning around and walking out of the cave.

They left the tunnel and two boys ran in with massive barrels; one of the boys placed one at the stone wall. The other boy standing at the door, opened a tap on the barrel and made a trail of the oil all the way back to the wall. He dropped it and they both ran out of the cave.

"Stand back", said the bomb man. He dropped another torch into the cave and it sparked the oil which caught fire. In a second it burnt through the tunnel until it burnt up to the barrels, and BANG! They exploded.

"Move", said Oring.

Eight knights this time ran in, four in front and four behind. In front they held shields and swords, the four behind had arrows ordered to shoot anything that moved.

Oring walked in and looked as the dust cleared, the tunnel was dark and the smell was worse.

"Claw with me, Clut when the tunnel is safe we'll send word for you to start sending people through", said Oring.

"Good luck", said Clut from the tunnel entrance.

The eight knights led the way slowly going forward pushing into the darkness. Behind them were two men with baskets full of torches. They walked on, every now and then they stabbed a torch in to the wall. Behind them was Oring, always with his hand on his sword, behind him was Claw and behind her were many more knights, men and ninja's.

They continued down the path until they came to a fork.

"Which way?" asked the front knight.

"Left", said Oring.

"Are you sure?" asked Claw.

"Yes", said Oring. They walked down to the left, as they went past they threw torches down the tunnel to light it up. Claw put six ninja's set in battle position to stand and guard the other path.

"Good luck", said Oring, hitting his hand down on one of them, looking back to the others.

They all walked and walked through the tunnel, stopping at every fork, blocking each with men to defend it. It took a couple of hours but they suddenly came to a turn, as they went round they found another stone wall.

"We're almost out, bring the bombs", said Oring.

The boys came back down and blew the wall off. As it crumbled the tunnel was filled with moonlight and the sound of the sea.

"We're through", said Oring. He walked out of the other side of the tunnel and they found themselves on a beach.

Oring looked around and to his left his saw the port of Potatar.

But then came a scream from the tunnel.

"Oh God!" said Oring pulling out his sword and running in to the tunnel. They came around a corner to see four dead men and a fifth pushing away a spider-like creature. It had the body of a man and the legs of a spider, on its face were eight evil beady eyes. It was completely covered in black fur and in its human hands it pushed a spear down killing the man. It turned to the knights and king.

"Go back to hell, you creature. Fire!" said Oring moving to the side, as three archers hit fire arrows, into the creature. The spider let out a cry as it started to burn. It leapt at Oring who answered with a blow from his sword slicing the spider's guts. It stumbled and fell on its back, all it's legs waving in the air. Oring walked around to its head where it took its final breath and said, "They will rise",.

"No they won't", said Oring, stabbing his sword down in to the spider's face.

"More men on this tunnel", said Oring, speed walking out of the cave and across the stone to the beach. Up to the port. There were wooden walls all around. Fire was lighting up the port, long large piers out in to the sea where many boats roped up and ready to use. Oring walked up to a large wooden door and he bashed on in BASH, BASH. A little wooden window shot open and a pair of eyes looked out, only to say "It's the king, open the door".

The little window closed and the doors were pulled open.

"Sir, what are you doing here?" asked the port master.

"We came by the tunnel", said Oring.

"The tunnel, but, sir…" said the port master, very anxious and putting a hand on his sword.

"Port master we have little time but we must move", said Oring. "I need your help again",

Minutes later, back in Vocar the city was filled with light and life, as the people prepared their things and started to walk through the tunnel. The knights helped pull the bags and pushed the animals as they walked through the tunnel and cave out the other side and walked across a now lit path, into Potatar. In the port they were quickly loaded into boats, sails were dropped and the boats, started to leave port.

"Send the boats, to this island we will re-group there", said Oring. For him and other boat captains stood around a table pointing at a map writing numbers and looking at the compass.

"Aye, sir", said the captains.

The night went along, but the number of people still in the city was high and Gergriff was closing fast. Oring and his best men were back at the castle on the front wall looking into the forest.

"Move the people faster, we're running out of time", said Oring.

"We can't move them any faster", said Sir Garrett

"We moved about half, sir", said Sir Worthing. Oring continued to look out until… Suddenly a great fireball shot up out of the forest and smashed down on the castle. Seconds later the Vikings made another charge at the castle this time with goblins, rocks and giants.

"Oh no", said Sir Worthing.

"Retreat, retreat. Move all men, defend the tunnel. We can hold them in the bottle neck", said Oring, running across the wall.

A horn was blown and the knights ran from the walls, people ran faster and moved quicker down the tunnel. Every knight and soldier moved to the front gates standing ready to defend.

The enemy was running at the castle, confused why they were not being rained on by arrows. They easily made their way to the gates and the giants started to punch and smash at the doors. The wood cracked but didn't move.

"Shields", said Oring. Standing back as a line of men walked forward and hook shield together in a long line.

"Archers", said Oring, behind the shield. Line after line of archers stood ready to fire.

"Stand ready", said Oring.

SMASH, CRUNCH went the door.

"Hold", said Oring again.

CRUNCH, SPLIT

"This is it: the last stand of Vocar. We saved the people but we cannot save her stone, not today. We will be back and we will win this WAR, FIRE!" shouted Oring.

A rain of arrows shot up, but the doors were locked. As they broke the arrow blasted through knocking back the enemy.

It didn't take them long to push the doors back open and charge in.

"For Vocar!" shouted Oring, running through the shields in to the enemy.

"For Vocar!" shouted the knights, as they ran in to battle with him, they ran but quickly, lost momentum as they started to get MUSHED AND MANGLED, PUSHED AND PULLED, CRUNCHED AND CRUSHED as the enemy broke their lines and ran throughout Vocar killing everyone in sight.

"Retreat!" shouted Oring. The knights split and ran throughout Vocar fighting for their lives. Hundreds were cornered and forced to surrender.

Oring and a handful of knights were pushed all the way back to the tunnel's door. Until Clut burst out of the tunnel with his captain elves shooting arrow after arrow.

"Sir the last of the people are through, as is most of the army, Claw is leading them", said Clut. All the people were through except for the many that were killed in the attack.

"We need to buy them more time, will you stand with me?" asked Oring.

"I will, uncle", said Clut.

So Oring and his nephew, with their last three knights and six elves stood in front of the tunnel facing all odds. Of course there were more knights and elves around the kingdom, over 2000 to be counting but most of them had been imprisoned.

A wave of goblins were coming at Origer and Clut. They both were armed and wasted no time to show off their moves in battle. They fought and killed, chopping up goblins left, right and centre. They battled with the heart of the dragon, killing with all their might, but even the strongest would never hold up to this barrage. The knights and elves fell, but soon Oring was smacked across the face and he fell.

"Uncle!" shouted Clut, cutting his way towards him but too late. As the sun set, Clut was knocked down.

Oring looked up at the goblins.

"Make it quick", said Oring closing his eyes.

"No, we have orders", said the goblin.

A cart pulled up and ropes were put out. All the surviving men's hands were tied and roped to a cart and they were pulled along.

They were pulled up to Gergriff sitting high on his horse.

"Oring, how the mighty have fallen", said Gergriff. Oring looked up at him and didn't say anything.

"What do you want?" asked Oring.

"Your stones", said Gergriff.

"Never, you mad man", said Oring, pulling himself to his full height, trying to look tall to Gergriff.

"How?" said Gergriff. He punched Oring across the face and sent Oring down in to the blood that traced the floors of Vocar.

"Sir", said two goblins, which were running up carrying the stone.

"The stones", said the goblin passing Gergriff the stone.

"Chest", said Gergriff.

A cart pulled up and a large chest, was taken out of the back and brought around to Gergriff. The large chest had a load of golden gears and cogs on the front.

"Put it down", said Gergriff, pointing to the floor. They placed it on the floor. Gergriff came up to it and waved his hand over the front lock and the gears and cogs all started to turn and twist as bolts were unlocked and the lid opened. Inside the chest were five slots carved out of the wood. Four were filled so Gergriff put it in the fifth, then they suddenly started to glow green.

"Excellent", said Gergriff.

He closed the lid and turned back to Oring.

"Bring them to the Wastes. We move now!" shouted Gergriff leaving on his horse.

Chapter 8
The Tree

We return now back to the forest, where we last left our heroes in a blue flash of light. Well the trees were filled with light and Origer, Beakey and Blike were gone.

"Hunt them down!" shouted King.

Now in another part of the forest inside a tree the blue light reappeared and the three of them found themselves in an untidy pile. A man stood there pointing a staff at them.

"Who are you?" asked the man.

"What?" asked Origer, looking up to the man. He had a brown beard down to his knees, and long purple robes. He had a silver belt and clips, he looked very Celtic, a Celtic wizard. He was holding a long wooden staff covered in the language of old Thringer and at the top was a green gem. This man over the age of 400 goes by the name Shamus.

"I say again, who you are?" asked Shamus.

"Who are you...?" asked Origer. He stopped for he had looked up.

Beakey and Blike both stood also looking up to their large surprise.

Remember I said they were inside a tree, a small tree on the outside but for the inside, it was huge, spiral staircases leading up and up, climbing all the way to the top. There were thousands of lights from candles, there were coloured gems giving out coloured lights. There were birds flying around carrying books. There were bookshelves everywhere, on each of them was a little bookworm sorting and reading and more sorting and more reading. Lots of coloured smoke and sparkling poles; there were paintings, paper, ten times as much as you'd find in a school. I could write book after book explaining Shamus's house but we must push on.

"I am Shamus, wizard of lightning and owner of the silver tree", said Shamus. "I will say one last time, who are you?".

"I am Prince Origer of the city of Vocar and these are Beakey and Blike", said Origer pointing to them.

"Vocar?" asked Shamus.

"Yes. Vocar, the city of men", said Origer.

"Then you might want to see this", said Shamus. He led them over to a table with a large green bowl filled with purple water.

He waved his hand over the bowl and muttered words.

Bowl of molar
Show me the city of Vocar
Give me
What I need to see
The city you must show
Or I will turn and go

As Shamus spoke, his voice was deep and strong as if he was echoing down a cave.

The water rippled and images started to form and show Vocar, but the great city, it was on fire, smoke broke from the castle, the streets were empty and the door was broken open.

"What? What happened to Vocar?" asked Origer staring in to the bowl.

"Vocar is in flames and the people have gone. Moved to a safe haven far from their city", said Shamus.

"What?" asked Origer.

"The people are safe", said Shamus.

"… What of my father?" asked Origer.

Shamus looked back in to the bowl.

"I don't know it's too… too much dark power, Gergriff has found the weapon of dark matter", said Shamus.

"What's that?" asked Origer.

"The weapon of dark matter…, bring the elemental book!" shouted Shamus. In a second two birds came up carrying a large book. They placed it on the table. Shamus pulled the cover and showed a page.

"The nine elemental weapons built to protect each of the kingdoms. Back then the kingdoms were not in races but in tribes instead.

At birth it would be chosen which tribe you would be brought up in, the tribes were

Fire – the tribe which trained dragons and were brought up with the powers of fire. Water – the peaceful tribe which flowed with water, not fighting but keeping peace. Rock – one of the strongest tribes who lived in caves and underground, training with great power. Wind – the real master of the air, living in the merciless mist. A mysterious tribe not on anyone's side, they fight for their own, never assisting. Ice – the cold tribe, savages of the land, but who have been lost in the frozen lands. Lightning – living high in the mountains, controlling storms and learning many skills of light. Steel – used by a master of the forge to create the greatest tools, but is not found, only made with the element of earth and fire. Life – only one person ever was chosen for the Life Tribe. Being the only one he was always outnumbered and on the run and in his final hour he left the sword of life trapped, fixed inside a rock only to be found again be someone with the power to master such a weapon. The only way to find this weapon is with the power of all of the elements combined.

But all of them were hidden by my great, great grandfather", said Shamus.

"That's only eight", said Blike.

"The last is the weapon of dark matter. In its day it was used by someone called the master but in the final days of The War Of Darkness he was sealed and forever trapped into a dark cloud. But now it seems Gergriff must be trying to bring him back to life", said Shamus.

"Yes… well", said Origer.

"Mr Wizard man did you fire that arrow?" asked Beakey who was not fully paying attention.

But just as he said that TWANG, an arrow hit the wall just above his head.

"That could have been messy", said a voice from up the stairs.

They all looked up to see two cloaked figures who jumped down and landed in the middle of them.

"We shot the arrow", said one of the men. They both took down their hoods to reveal that they were both elves, elf twins. Both had black long hair and long dark blue cloaks, silver belts and white arrow quiver on their backs, long very impressive bows with many engravings and suchlike.

"Who are you?" asked Beakey pulling the arrow out of the wall.

"These are my warriors", said Shamus.

They all looked at him more confused than before.

"I hired them to rescue a thing that I'd lost throughout the forest. By the way did you find it?" asked Shamus.

"No", said Larry.

I forgot to say their names are Barry and Larry or was it Larry then Barry?. Anyway back to business, both of them elves.

"No luck, these guys got in the way", said Barry.

"I need that flower", said Shamus.

"Elves", said Beakey turning very angry.

"Who are you?" asked Barry.

"That's none of your business, elves", said Beakey.

"Oh, yes", said Larry putting his hand on his sword.

"I won't go there", said Beakey drawing his sword.

"I will", said Larry, he quickly drew his sword and took a swing at Beakey. He was about to attack back, but Shamus smashed his staff into the ground creating a flash and pushed both Larry and Beakey to walls on each side.

"There will be no bloodshed in this tree", said Shamus.

"I hate elves", said Beakey.

"Why?" asked Larry.

"Because I fought on the coast of the Handel, in the battle of the rush gun", said Beakey dropping down from the wall.

"Oh", said Larry as he fell silent.

For you who don't know, the battle of the rush gun, took place at the heart of the Handel Islands. The pirates were trapped in a small castle built on an island, they were cut off, no food, no water and no way of escape. The Viking fleet had them pinned to the Handel fortress. Over 800 pirates were killed and the elves only stood and watched. It was called the rush gun because of the cannons and how fast they were loaded and fired.

The room was still silent until."What flower, you mentioned?" asked Origer turning back to their old talk.

"The Trec king has a staff with a glass ball in the top, Shamus needs it", said Larry.

"Why?" asked Origer.

"Another book will be needed", said Shamus. He called out again and more birds brought him another book. He opened it and put on his reading glasses. Shamus loved to tell tales to anyone and everyone.

"200 years after Thringer was formed the five wizards were sent to stop evil from entering the world. Until they came to the Snake War. A great battle arose in this forest and the five wizards were killed. But as they died they each left a part of their soul in five flowers and those flowers were kept in a glass ball for many ages. Being passed down and down until they came to me. But on my travels I was attacked and one of the flowers was taken." Shamus walked to the other side of the room and opened a large metal cabinet. Inside there lay four glass balls, each with a flower prettier than the last inside each of them.

"I have four, the Trec king has the fifth, I need it back so I hired these two to retrieve it", said Shamus.

"Right, with you now", said Origer, still confused but he had the gist of it.

"Well, this has all been good fun but we must push on", said Blike. He turned and started to push Beakey.

"Come on let's go", said Blike.

"We can't go yet", said Origer.

"Why?" asked Blike.

"We've lost the path", said Origer.

"Ah… that is a problem", said Blike.

"Do you know the way to the other side of the forest?" said Origer.

"Yes I do", said Shamus.

"Great, which way?" asked Origer.

"I won't say I have a task for you", said Shamus.

"What?" asked Origer.

Chapter 9

The quest inside the quest

Next thing they knew Shamus had persuaded the five of them to retrieve the flower. Beakey and Larry had both come to an agreement, they wouldn't kill each other.

"This is mad", said Origer as the five of them walked through the forest.

"Mad, how?" asked Larry.

"We're risking our lives to find a flower", said Origer.

"Shamus did promise to show us the way out of the forest, plus he said there'll be gold to go along with it", said Beakey.

"I still think it ma…" said Origer but couldn't finish for Larry slapped a hand over his mouth. The five stopped and looked up again at the same large mess of wooden planks, ropes and Trec's. A giant ant-like nest hanging from the trees.

The five of them hid down in the bushes and looked up at the nest.

"What's the plan?" asked Blike.

"Well it's better that there's five of us, last time there was only two, so this whole thing is held up by those", said Larry pointing to the largest tree which had hundreds of ropes coming from it which spread through the trees, the biggest tree was just above the king's thorn.

"That hold's it up, Beakey and Blike you will destroy it", said Larry.

"Barry this is our escape plan", said Larry giving his brother an arrow with a purple crystal sticking out of the end.

"Origer, you and I will talk to the king, I will distract him while you grab the ball", said Larry.

"Right", said Origer.

"You three go, cut the ropes, then jump down with Barry, break the arrow and Bob's your uncle", said Larry.

"Our uncle's name is Fred", said Barry.

"It's an expression", said Larry.

"Right", said Barry. He, Blike and Beakey walked keeping their heads down. They ran from tree to tree, bush to bush.

"Let's go", said Larry, running into the thick bushes.

"Wait for me", said Origer running after them.

They found a rope and they climbed up it onto the nest. They ran for cover and Larry popped up his head, as did Origer before being pushed down as a Trec walked past, Larry jumped up, took out a sword and placed it on the Trec's neck.

"Take us to your leader", said Larry.

Next thing that they knew, sorry to rush but they walked a long way. They were standing in front of the king and all around them were Trec's laughing. The king letting out a dreadful cackle.

"Why would you come back, you fools?" said King.

"Well… no lies, we come to steal that", said Larry pointing at king's staff.

"What do you want it for?" asked King.

"It's needed for a friend", said Larry looking back at Origer.

"You can't have it", said King.

"Why?" asked Larry. At this point Origer was slowly walking around. Also at this point Beakey and Blike with Barry were climbing up the tree to the rope wheel; they pulled themselves to the top.

"That was a long way", said Beakey looking down.

"Beakey?" asked Blike just getting up with Barry behind him.

"Wha…" stopped Beakey. For he turned around to find Trec's coming right at Beakey.

Beakey drew and the three of them charged into the fight cutting down the Trecs. Making their way to the ropes.

"Now which one do we cut?" said Blike pulling out a knife.

"Not yet", said Barry. He was looking down on Origer and Larry talking, they could just about hear, but let's go back down.

"200 golden pieces", said Larry. Origer was still walking around as Larry tried to get the king to take money.

"5000", said King.

"1000", said Larry.

"3000", said King.

"200", said Larry.

"10000", said King.

"What! That's madness, why do you even need money?" said Larry.

"We don't? Wait a minute, we don't. Kill them!" shouted King.

Origer and Larry jumped back to back holding swords and stood ready as the Trec's around were armed and ready.

"What now?" asked Origer.

"Time to go", said Larry. "Now!" he shouted up to Barry.

"Go!" shouted Barry.

"Go, which go?" said Blike looking at all the ropes.

"Do all the goes", said Beakey. He picked up one of the Trec's axes. Blike ducked as Beakey swung and sliced the axe into the ropes: SNAP, PING, SLICE, SMASH. The ropes broke and the nest started to shake and break and fall to the ground. The platform that Larry and Origer were on shook and wobbled. Origer jumped, cut the king's staff and took the glass ball.

"Barry!" shouted Origer defending off the king. The king came at him swinging his staff up and down.

"Right, time to go", said Barry. He pulled out the arrow, Blike and Beakey started to climb down quickly, as Barry stumble with his arrow and then WHOOPS it slipped and left his hand.

"Oh no" the arrow fell and hit the tree and then another tree before falling into the darkness of the forest. Everyone looked as it went, even Shamus was looking in his bowl of water.

"Barry!, I must rescue them" said Shamus. He walked back and looked up at his tree home; he clicked his fingers and a brown sack fell and landed flat in front of him.

You my home
Will go to this dome
Put yourself in this sack
I promise you'll be back
The bag of depths
Filled with space
Bring everything even my mace
We will leave now
Come or be eaten by a cow

The words were said and he bashed his staff on the ground and the crystal in the end started to glow.

The tree fell silent until the bag started to move, it floated up in front of Shamus. It opened itself and a long beam of light shot up into the air. A shaft of light no thicker than a cup started to spin with great speed. Around and around it went creating a wind. Not a danger or violent wind but a safe soft wind. The wind started to pull books off shelves and bottles off tables, papers and paint were all pulled in, even the logs in the fire still alight, the birds, the worms, everything, except Shamus and the bag; they were the only things left in the room.

"That was fun", said Shamus. He grabbed the bag, put it over his shoulder and went out of the house, he stood outside and spoke more magic.

A horse I will need
Send me a horse from Gleed
The horse of the light forces
I need him of course

For this he didn't bang his staff, he clicked his fingers and a bright ball of light filled the forest and a blue horse charged out. Not a normal horse but a blue horse.

"Good to see you again", said Shamus. He quickly roped up a cart and jumped up. He whipped the reign and was off as fast as the horse could take him.

Not far from there on a falling platform, Origer and Larry were fighting off the Trec King. While Beakey and Blike just got down on to the same platform to catch Barry who fell.

"You dozy prawn", said Blike pulling Barry to his feet.

"Don't fight now, there's no time", said Beakey, falling about like a horse on ice. The platform was swaying from side to side, swaying in the wind like a leaf on a tree in winter, it will eventually fall.

"What's the plan?!" shouted Blike.

"Don't know", said Larry. Origer and Larry were being battered by the King. Until FOOSH an arrow shot into the back of the king's head, sticking out the front. Origer and Larry stopped as the king fell and Beakey was behind holding his bow.

"Come on, guy's, go for the head", said Beakey.

"So what are we going to do?" said Blike wobbling over.

"Urr…?" said Origer then he started to see the planks that they were on starting to break apart.

"Run", suggested Barry.

"Run", said Larry.

They started to run off along the planks but the planks started to break and it wasn't long before the Trec's started to come after them. They jumped in only to be chopped to bits. They continued running and slicing their way along the paths. Ropes were breaking, planks were falling, Trec's were jumping and Beakey was laughing as he shot arrow after arrow.

They sprinted faster and faster but they were unaware that they were climbing higher and higher until… they found the end of the path.

Origer in front looking down as the Trec hoards were running after them.

"Go, Origer", said Larry.

"No more path", said Origer.

They all turned and started to defend against the Trec's. Blike and Beakey would hit them, and push them back in to Origer's sword or Larry would give Barry a leg up to come down quick with a slice across the neck.

They were being pushed closer to the edge until a yell came.

"Ahoy!" shouted Shamus. He was running across the forest floor.

"Come on", said Shamus riding under their path.

"It's a long drop", said Barry.

"You'll live", said Larry pushing him and then jumping himself.

Each person jumped and swung on ropes, they dropped in or next to the cart.

"Ay up what are you doing here?" asked Beakey.

"I thought you might need help", said Shamus.

"Well you better start giving it", said Origer as an arrow hit in to his bag.

The Trec's dropped from the trees, running after them shooting arrows.

"Take them down", said Shamus. He opened his bag and pulled out several sets of arrows and bows.

Blike, Beakey, Origer, Barry and Larry shot arrow after arrow off the cart hitting Trec after Trec. But then suddenly the Trec's stopped running and just watched.

"Why are they stopping?" said Shamus, now in the cart and not on the horse.

"Shamus who's driving?" asked Origer.

"I am", said Shamus.

All five of them looked back as the cart was heading for a cliff edge. Shamus tried to pull back but it was too late, the cart launched off the cliff edge…

To be continued

Rate this book on our website!

www.novum-publishing.co.uk

The author

J.N.S. Pluckrose lives in Plymouth in the UK where as well as enjoying the adventure of being a first-time novelist, he also enjoys baking for his family. In addition to his work as an author, James is training to be a caterer.

novum 🔹 PUBLISHER FOR NEW AUTHORS

The publisher

*He who stops
being better
stops being good.*

This is the motto of novum publishing, and our focus is on finding new manuscripts, publishing them and offering long-term support to the authors.
Our publishing house was founded in 1997, and since then it has become THE expert for new authors and has won numerous awards.

Our editorial team will peruse each manuscript within a few weeks free of charge and without obligation.

You will find more information about
novum publishing and our books on the internet:

w w w . n o v u m - p u b l i s h i n g . c o . u k